Olympic

John L. Miller

A Publication of The Poetry Box®

Poems ©2022 John L. Miller
All rights reserved.

Editing, Book & Cover Design: Shawn Aveningo Sanders

No part of this book may be reproduced in any manner whatsoever without permission from the author, except in the case of brief quotations embodied in critical essays, reviews and articles.

ISBN: 978-1-956285-09-3
Printed in the United States of America.
Wholesale Distribution via Ingram.

Published by The Poetry Box®, June 2022
Portland, Oregon
ThePoetryBox.com

To my Nicole, without whose strength and partnership in marriage I would not have found myself in Portland, or authentically become a writer.

To every poet and writer I have met, who has passed through, stayed around, or left too soon.

*Después de este desorden impuesto, de esta prisa,
de esta urgente gramática necesaria en que vivo,
vuelva a mí toda virgen la palabra precisa,
virgen el verbo exacto con el justo adjetivo.*

After this willful derangement, this harassed
and necessitous grammar by whose haste I must live,
let the virginal word come back to me whole and meticulous,
and the virginal verb, justly placed with its rigorous adjective.

—an excerpt from
"*De ayer para hoy*" ("From Yesterday for Today")
by Rafael Alberti, translated by Ben Belitt

Poems

7	|	A Diasia
8	|	Cronus
9	|	Hermes
10	|	Aphrodite
11	|	Aeneas
13	|	Eris
15	|	Three Mysteries
16	|	Demeter: April 2020
17	|	Adonis
18	|	Circe: October 2020
19	|	Hypnos
20	|	Atlas
22	|	Pandora
24	|	Poseidon
26	|	Helen
28	|	Odysseus
29	|	Heracles
31	|	Icarus
32	|	Niobe
34	|	Minotaur
36	|	Bellerophon Considers the Winged Horse
38	|	Perseus
40	|	The Marriage of Perseus and Andromeda
42	|	Achilles
43	|	Scylla
45	|	Cup Foods
47	|	Tantalus
48	|	Medusa

A Diasia

I hope I have this right—after fasting all day,
there should be a feast. But that night
the animal's burnt whole,

to a charred husk of the inedible.
It's the time of year:
hunger that needs memory, lived experience,

spirit as all want, indelible and worsened.
The fire deepens.
Through smoke, fumes,

morning, the next day, where a silence
bars every door.
But inside there is bread or cake,

tea that waits to settle despair.
In warming noon air, consider
the groom to a path, the stack to a wall,
hills leveled or left to stand.

For every victory, nothing happens
without first working together.
Carefully pouring one cup,
giving that cup to one other,

thirst that brings on work of alliance.
But before city or state: there must be
a father, a mother.

Cronus

> *In revenge, Mother Earth persuaded the Titans to attack their father; and they did so, led by Cronus, the youngest of the seven, whom she armed with a flint sickle.*

There are stories and liars about my father,
probably with a sickle in his left hand,
his body tight with the act,
in the aftermath his breath
an upheaval of victory thrown to the stars,

as a crow watches,
fat with winter,
black feathers gleaming and oracular.

My father so desperate to see what he might not,
he disgorges the ordinary stone, caught out
in his endless appetite for rejection—

how far back does the cycle go?
Believe those who say
my mother protected me.

But the notion that nothing that comes
comes from one
wakes me now
cold under covers.

I am alone for the latest time
caught again with searching
for everything not kept in heaven.

Morning comes with the car still here,
the yard empty, the day racing with the death of the year.

A door to you—closed
that I try but
I don't know how to open.

Hermes

> *"Then make me your herald, Father," Hermes answered,*
> *"and I will be responsible for the safety of all divine*
> *property, and never tell lies, though I cannot promise*
> *always to tell the whole truth."*

On payday Fridays you make it a habit
to bring your son a pack of chewing gum,
pack of crayons, a Matchbox car.

You watch his hands grasp,
eyes traveling over corners.
He takes his time, or he never unwraps

to get to the sticks, the colors, or the car inside.
His eyes tell you it's out of fear
of ruining newness and perfection.

You are teaching him what's precious, the exact
and aspiration that is becoming this country.
Watch him receive, accumulate, secret away—

your son's imperfect way of collecting,
though his eyes never ask when
might there be more.

It's only surprise after surprise of divine property—
they are small gifts, but at every two weeks
a big cut of his life to wait.

Forgive your son for forgetting.

Aphrodite

> *When they parted at dawn, she revealed her identity, and made him promise not to tell anyone that she had slept with him. Anchises was horrified to learn that he had uncovered the nakedness of a goddess and begged her to spare his life.*

(The slightest turn)

                the early morning

turn away

                a guilt

return to it

                feels like truth

go back and forth

                prove love as
                unremunerated labor

the myrtle, the rose, the sparrow,

                the durable, the delicate

scallop shells, dolphins

                permanence, the ephemeral

born with it

                already knowing

forgiven

                the trappings

entrapment

                a golden throne

unfaithful

                alive

Aeneas

> *Aeneas proved a skilled fighter and even Achilles did not
> disparage him: for if Hector was the hand of the Trojans,
> Aeneas was their soul.*

I can be a city father the way my father
was just a man on a hill,

until the bolt came down
and made him, from me, some agent of history.

Look around now, all the fallen and dead,
the wrecked, the burning:

I am still here. I run my hand over the scar
from a spear that should have killed me,

or was it an arrow—I don't remember.
It's not the sky I look to for an answer.

I just do,
somewhat what's told me,

some of how I'm trusted,
some that comes spoken or gestured in dreams.

I threaten to lose everything to war.

What will endure past my time

may not be up to me, and what is my time,
after the chase,

the conniving, the campaigns,
the stories that have me climbing to heaven?

[. . .]

I am still here. My father had me
and all the greatest pleasures.

I have this world.
I soften my gaze at the gray, taken back again

to carrying him over my shoulder.
Breathe in terror

evident in the fact of the sack of a city.
What exactly is tomorrow?
Ask again. Ask again.

Eris

> *Thereupon Zeus, aided by Eris, reversed the laws of
> Nature, which hitherto had been immutable.*

The tree limb hangs
by a wire,

u-bolt anchored, rusted but strong.
At a distance looks floating in space,

taking languid turns
in the early morning.

The other limbs crack sap scent into the air,
spill
split on the neighbor's driveway,

a length and canopy rich with needles,
needles ending in tiny flowers.

Their weight and rush of falling
what I slept through, as if a lightness,

a secret
not a sizzling, severed power line,

not a smashed
parked car.

It required no lights
no sirens,

no startling awake
walking out to find disaster—

mislead me,
faith—

make me think I need to thank
for the near miss of a huge thing.

Three Mysteries

> *And the poet moves slowly looking at the stones*
> *and asks*
> *I wonder do they exist*
> —George Seferis

a young woman in all black
in brightly colored hair

pushes a wheeled bag
on broken sidewalk

walks in stockinged feet

and

an apartment courtyard
in high summer

honeybees

hundreds
in thick low dry grass

from one withered
dandelion
to another

and

Demeter: April, 2020

> *Demeter was so angry that, instead of returning to Olympus, she continued to wander about the earth, forbidding the trees to yield fruit and the herbs to grow, until the race of men stood in danger of extinction.*

I am here speaking on Demeter,
on the creation of winter,

which no longer has to do with the weather.
Outside looks like the burgeoning of any spring,

but I don't know if there was another abduction.
We're here, and bargaining,

and with so many already dead. Yes, they suffered,
and they matter as much as her daughter,

and so far, your lot indifferent
as our world filled with sirens and crying out,

with quiet resignation, with seething. It's all deafening.
All this time waiting for a wrong kind of change

to be made right—is it to you we ask?
I am ready with fruit, with any red seed needed,

if that's what needs. But I need to know
about your Olympian conferences,

your decisions. Our stories of you,
those would die, too. It's no threat,

it's real. That's how much this time
is different, it's urgent,

I'm pleading,
please.

Adonis

> *the pomegranate was supposed to have sprung—like*
> *the eight-petalled scarlet anemone—from the blood of*
> *Adonis...*

the only time you and I have seen such a press

it was in Istanbul

it was like two palms of two hands
come down with fingers laced

to drench red juice from the large fruit
into its rimmed catch below

and by its single lip
pour into a single glass

become what we've never tasted again

the sidewalk winds
wraps around memory

zagging streets
middle of the city of the known world
ever since the boar

possessed by immortality
charged and killed him

ever since his mother
split open as a myrrh tree
bore him

the beauty that brings bounty
that can look everlasting

but can come to be dangerously ignored.

Circe: October 2020

> *The goddess set a mess of cheese, barley, honey, and wine before the hungry sailors; but it was drugged, and no sooner had they begun to eat than she struck their shoulders with her wand and transformed them into hogs.*

Surely, they're rogues turned into animals, stuffed into good suits fit to aging bodies. With close-cropped haircuts, towel-dried, combed over, they leave in the dark to come back in the dark, spending hours in between in congress or at the Capitol, under bright lights, under the rutting of questioning, pronouncing confidence in smooth language daily—look, if she's been around she's been busy, turning leaders, voters, whole cities menagerie. Where her spell ends perhaps no one knows—there's a reason they once marooned her, hid her in thickets of alder—she's out and about today where there are countries, wide and flat, close to the size of continents—I mean, what is distance, or millions, billions, elections, anticipating, happening or beginning or ending to her weight of sadness, of rage, wandering and wanting, her fate a plaything, her never-mending heart carrying knowledge of love, never receiving it.

Hypnos

> *Zeus awoke in a rage and threatened to cast Sleep
> down from the upper air into the gulf of Erebus;
> but she fled as a suppliant to Night, whom even
> Zeus dared not displease.*

My mother tries to put me to sleep,
leading by the hand, into the room.

Trégua, she says, suggesting a fatigue with living
rest for which comes only at the end,

and what could I know, at its beginning?
She turns out one light, but not the other.

Outside, at a distance, a radio tower—
it flashes a red beacon, during the day

imperceptible, but at night—it faces me when in bed,
blinks at me piercingly,

demands something I cannot offer.

I've asked through the window before,

before falling into the cave,
but I've never discerned an answer.

It's so a plane won't crash into it,
she told me once, and in the next breath,

to try and dream before leaving.

Atlas

> *Gigantic Atlas, eldest of the brothers, knew all the depths of the sea; he ruled over a kingdom with a precipitous coastline, larger than Africa and Asia put together. This land of Atlantis lay beyond the Pillars of Heracles...*

You wear the armillary pinpricks of heaven
forever. You are faced in true direction,
north. Somehow you do not fall,
do not fail. Your one foot

yet to gain purchase, the other
already slipping off: your punishment
is not the weight: it's forever to lack
leverage. Your body argues an argument

lost to time. I looked up at you as we
walked into the International Building;
past the cobbler, the barber, the studio
for two-inch square photographs,

into the State Department Passport Office
for my first blue book of citizenship.
It's taken my life to now to discern your fate
as the extinguishment of desire,

that from announcement of your sentence
every moment would be one of devotion
to the warding off of total loss.
Such was the fragility to their immigrants' arrival,

to mine as American. Such were the stakes.
With my eyes now but remembering
as a child, I look up at my mother and father,
their faces a glare of spring sun,

and I could ask without speaking:
Do you know what you've done?
Are you ready?

Pandora

> *In World War II I was a bombardier based in Italy.*
> *I was on the American side but let me assure you the*
> *history books are right. We won. If you had seen me*
> *bomb, you would have doubts.*
>   *I was the world's worst.*
>   —Richard Hugo

If all you are is back in Phillipsburg, Montana,
you consider that a gift.
Boredom enough, but think of the quiet there, too,
the clarity of nothing today, nothing
tomorrow. But there is or can be so much
in the stillness of ruin.
Regret in gray knitted into the sky,
pulled into the ground, bricked into buildings,
settling into the people around you, into you.

Elsewhere is the blessing of not-you.
You are here. Not dancing, no one is,
but sitting, drinking, watching the front door
open occasionally, snatch the afternoon inside.
Anywhere like Phillipsburg takes you
back to Italy, to 1945,
to the first monstrous consequences
you took responsibility for,
then your racing away since,
at four-engine speed,

five miles up, barely willing. You are grateful
for cloud cover, thinking or trying to over the roar,
looking at the night's payload
expectant in the bomber's bay,
masses of dark and what each of them,
all of them, would do.

The idea that masses behind your eyes:
that they are the winged souls, waiting,
anxious to fly.
That they belong to you.
You look at your hand.
You would open those doors.

Poseidon

> *He boasts of having created the horse…and of having invented the bridle…but his claim to have initiated horse racing is undisputed.*

the lots out of the helmet were fair
                                  and there were three of you

the world could have been anything then
                               and good

                but lo
your unhappiness

           to be the one boxed in
but on the bridle

                       trying to push out from within
                       a manic parade of silks

who would guess you in the crowd as one of the punters
                 a regular
trident to a cane

                          your passion the choice mare

barely at your seat for the winner
                   you want to ride the echo
                   of the loudspeaker's announcements

    winnings are always more than money

                                      your brothers such suckers

                                      out of your father's murder

    you should have gotten more

    ever since

                                      chasing irrecoverable looks
                                      just like the sea

    doubling down

               doubling down

                          winner

                          leader

                          stallion

    father had everything

                          let the three of you throw it all away

                          the more you think about it

    the more you come down to you

                                      of course
                                      no one sees it that way

Helen

> *When Helen, Leda's beautiful daughter, grew to womanhood at Sparta in the palace of her foster-father Tyndareus, all the princes of Greece came with rich gifts as her suitors, or sent their kinsmen to represent them.*

My father, by Odysseus' trusted counsel,
accepts each gift proffered,
in return draws the other closer, offers in his whisper
a few words to each man.

I cannot hear what's said,
words losing themselves to the air,
but in each whisper's soft hiss,
with kiss of agreement,
I suspect

each man has been told and offered
the same. I woke this morning told
to dress and stand
and their gaze—

each man looks an arrow at me
from across the room. They enter
even and serious but when provoked
by my father's sub rosa spell

each man, as each leaves,
looks at me like shattering windows.
I'm nauseous that agreement
resolves to possession,

each man
to be brought a piece of me, my body no more
than bargained jointing of a horse.

What else, where else, who else? I ask myself
in the silence between each man,
my own gaze steady.
I at least have learned, father,

an appearance of not knowing.
But if I could, would I, and what?
Who is asking these questions? I don't know.
Or I already know.

Each man will split, opened at his chest
with his own measure
of the great, coming tragedy.
Behind my eyes moves in the edge of the wide world.
Someone is telling a story that can't be heard
but I listen to with my whole body.

Duty is what each man will tell me it is.
But what is love? My heart is told
that story cannot wait. That whisper
racing in my ear!

Odysseus

> *Odysseus had been warned by an oracle: 'If you go to Troy, you will not return until the twentieth year, and then alone and destitute.'*

what to do with that guy you see everywhere,
the one who's done everything,

whose "y" in their name's
become default for far-ranging,

for taking so long, forgotten and forgetful,
that he comes back a different guy,

having lived different lives,
become not what he started but how it ends,

when there's as little peace having done too much
as having done nothing,

life proven as not a balance,
but a push

through decision after decision,
which comes to look more reckless than deliberate,

more circumstance than design.
But all the way in back of mind that counsel, once:

*Look, guy,
what else will you do?*

*You tried clowning at insanity,
but there is no returning to what you had.*

*Agamemnon is raising an army.
You're here now.*

*You will need all your rage.
You will need your cleverness.*

Heracles

> *Yet while the immortal Heracles banquets at the divine table, his mortal phantom stalks about Tartarus, among the twittering dead...*

Given such gifts, and height,
and strength; promised land,
seed, and weather;

he would see the whole sky
littered with his sex,
his deaths, all except his own,

reading his future among the hurl of stars
he would say flung on his behalf:
what does he accept as enough?

Never sought for wisdom,
his power not in self-reflection,
that recklessness of his virtue

when the world is new and wild.
But what happens after all around him age,
after a hundred bulls,

the dying down of laughter,
a murder of friends?
He says such a life is unimaginable,

to be cursed with blood boiling,
his shirt taking his skin with it.
The earth rending with his pain,

clearly, he would take the world with him first—
and so
the spectacle of the pyre,

[. . .]

the carefully placed kindling,
politic gifts ensuring immortality—
is this like love,

a drifting from ideal toward greed?
Revealed as not as blessed,
persistent through ignorance after ignorance,

ending like the sky or ocean,
feeling only at the end
beset with consequence.

Icarus

> *As Icarus and Daedalus sped away from the island*
> *in a north-easterly direction, flapping their wings,*
> *the fishermen, shepherds, and ploughmen who gazed*
> *upwards mistook them for gods.*

Every time our phone rang, every
request for money—you would converse,
then agree to send twenty dollars, or fifty. They insist

the amount changes my grandmother's, my grandfather's lives,
but not enough to save or stop them from calling.
Every month another call,

and whatever love you felt sours—
I saw it in your shoulders, at your back,
every time ringing irrupted from the wall,

what I saw, what phone calls became,
what they are now. Did you warn me? Did I
ignore it? Have I gone along too far, too high,

too late see in a sun the price of missing
what could be asked, what could be given?
You might have tried, but I now know

we both have returned in mind again to the labyrinth,
come back to what you built, or what you,
with guilt, couldn't bear leaving.

Even with doomed wings, headstrong,
the sky remains before me, like what Icarus would believe,
up to the fatal height where I am this: begun to fly.

Niobe

> *The statue of Niobe is a crag of roughly human shape, which seems to weep when the sun's arrows strike its winter cap of snow…*

I don't want to talk about it.
No one does.

Or no one talks about it

because many of us
have let ourselves be turned
into stone Thebans.

It can be easy
not to care,
not to wonder

where it came from,
who said it
first, where or who

or what it injures.

Easier than
pleading your case

in the arrows' face,
as if arrows could speak,
as if they could adjudicate.

Let this face
become a hastened temple.
Let her become ours.

Ask how to save yourself—
leadership appears

out of a throng, knowing nothing
but song and song.
The drone of it, sycophancy!

Many in our elected body
believe prayers go up to Heaven,
but they're wrong,

including that they're prayers.
The poisoned words begin and exist,
move outward from one.

Its start is imperceptible
against the humility
of being lost for words.

But for you they come.
They will hollow out your center.

Minotaur

> *This Minotaur, whose name was Asterius, or Asterion, was the bull-headed monster which Pasiphaë had borne to the white bull.*

Mother,
      I think of you often—
though I don't bother saying it,
not to the walls, not to the darkness.
Why? Because moving or not moving
is where I am. I forget my body is how I am.
I can breathe and walk but when others approach,
holding thin light if survived,
their tired hands holding it,

they turn mute at first sight of me.
I don't speak on that hunger, not anymore.
What happens, happens without echo.
If I stand straight up, I brush the ceiling.
My arms straight out touch opposite walls.
Though my feet don't yet know
each grain of dirt, all they know is dirt.
It appears I know everything.

               Mother,
the only thing I really see is fear.
For it, I recognize the smallest differences—they arrive wounded,
with a glazed resignation numbed by wine;
rarely, they have a willingness to fight
with whatever's left of themselves.
I am expert in that moment,
the moment after, and nothing else.

But with any variety, I learn.
I have years between lessons.
I learn down to the grain, the seam,

the air of it. With every step I take
I go where only I have been.
I teach myself about bone,

                  Mother,
where no one else has been.
If you could see. What disturbs
about cleaning and drying them disappears.
The first circle grew into several.
I converse with their empty faces.
Their teeth a careful adornment in the dirt,
I step through, remembering placement,
molar. I am tracing a way with lengths of leg
to see if I can find a center, or an end.

The passages here go for turn and curve, curve and turn—
I've never found where they end.
Yet I know where to go and how to return
when hunger summons. Where to find them.
Today is one of their days—I can smell their sweat.
This one…bears the scent of a plan,
carries something, believes in it.
The air moves with them, toward me. I breathe.
I watch my world flicker.
I do enjoy the light.

Bellerophon Considers the Winged Horse

> *Bellerophon, at the height of his fortune, presumptuously undertook a flight to Olympus, as though he were an immortal; but Zeus sent a gadfly, which stung Pegasus under the tail, making him rear and fling Bellerophon ingloriously to earth.*

The question as found or lost

                     trailed in wellspring

The landscape in water
               in distance as purpose
or escape as circuit

           The world
as what's lost in asking

The question this rider

looking for a ride

         finding it

      having answer as a golden saddle to throw over

losing it

      The ride stung by the gadfly

you're thrown

          Purpose this rider
            never understanding the ride

wanting it or taking it or living it down

Look at them

      the distances

from one shore to another

                Depths

the question that can give so much

that can leave you lame

Perseus

how a gene, when pulled, unravels a child
—Torin Greathouse

The gene, pulled,
unravels inside the candle, pull
of the wick on wax.

Flame, like Perseus, unknowing,
keyed knowledge
of immediate need,

how much for it might be left.
What's most difficult? Leaving,
like from an era or age. Acrisius,

fighting the future—
why anyone believes the future
belongs to them

must make the gods laugh.
Laughter the length of the sky,
an ouroboros, beginning,

ending, beginning, ending,
forever ending
according to the book

or story to which you devote.
I prefer the fatal swell of Helios. I
imagine the scale of devouring,

the turn to dreamless black
already in night clouds, flat black
moment that ends

any question of what then.
Well, incalculable silence, and then,
belief; then, long after,

spark of what's next.
What to do with next time?
Pull along what we think we know.

What we can.
Light the new candle.
Promise to that candle all this new flame.

The Wedding of Perseus and Andromeda

> *In the ensuing fight, Perseus struck down many of his opponents but, being greatly outnumbered, was forced to snatch the Gorgon's head from its bed of coral and turn the remaining two hundred of them to stone.*

All at once, the wedding party froze.
Two hundred caught in every shove, punch,
rush toward or away this wreck of ceremony.

Cups finished falling and shattering,
tables splitting and splintering, sounds
trailing to turn strange and single.

The air stayed rank with wine
and live hot breath, but bodies and faces
turned to nothing as a mountainside.

Even when broken, you warned me last night,
the chains are still there. You are calm,
holding the dead-snaked head, and my hand.

You say, these are just men.
You have entreated with gods
for the power of this moment—your winged sandals,

the prize of the Gorgon.
You say you live as proof.
I look over to the granite of my mother and father.

Why couldn't you leave well enough alone? I ask.
You both had your plans, even left me for the sea,
but then I met this husband of happenstance.

You both will be thrown to the stars.
There will be nothing I can do
to change their resulting unkindness.

My husband and I turn to leave.
I ask that before we fly, we walk slowly.
The first hour of our marriage is this now-quiet field.

A breeze winds its way through the new statuary,
the sun starting its daily work of shadow.
I can see grass already sprouting at the foot of them.

The later years of trees will make this place
nowhere. Forgive me, I say to him—
it may be too long before I feel.

Achilles

> *But Achilles, on hearing the news, rolled in the dust,*
> *and yielded to an ecstasy of grief.*

The news today I choose to bear

        Shortly I will flee the city for elsewhere

The city then not the same as today's

        that swell and surge of saying

grief becomes terror at my heart's walls

        changes what's inside too much like undoing

It wants to roll in the dust

        It wants to be its ecstasy of grief

in its loneliness wants me to come with it

        I say no

I say yes

        It is a thrum at the gates

persisting all night

        I try to turn to it

in turning I turn away

Scylla

> *Scylla, however, swam after his ship, and clung to the stern until her father Nisus's soul in the form of a sea-eagle swooped down upon her...*

She asked me if I loved her as I washed dishes.
She and I, some evenings together,
an afternoon or two, and sometime within the few
she confessed her father

had wanted her aborted,
and that she'd been kicked out of Binghamton
not from illness like she first confessed,
but a fistfight,

a pill bottle, waking up
handcuffed to a hospital bed.
Then moving in with her mother in Sheepshead Bay,
then moving in with her father in Prospect Heights,

finding nothing in between
except straits of being nineteen,
to have become to this grown man
somehow love's body but not its tongue,

because he said little except *I'll keep listening*,
dark-eyed Minos
leaving questions of her eyes
to silence. How he would persist that night

and another night and for months still,
making out of the two of them
and as if for her
a trireme to sail away

[. . .]

from being alone, but never getting past
the moment without future,
which made her measure again
about drowning again.

Cup Foods
-for George Floyd

> But the West Wind had also taken a fancy to
> Hyacinthus, and became insanely jealous of Apollo, who
> was one day teaching the boy how to hurl a discus, when
> the West Wind caught it in mid-air, dashed it against
> Hyacinthus's skull, and killed him. From his blood
> sprang the hyacinth flower, on which his initial letters
> are still to be traced

Here, where I am in the Northwest,
it's Eurus we fear, east wind that by September
blows around our home dried to a cinder,
ashes from a million annual acres some years,
a direction we orient interior,
passive sins of origin, pioneer myth.
Somewhere a shore without invader. But here,

we welcome Zephyrus, off the ocean,
often potent, often gentle, blankets of snow,
steady rain of miracles—
inviting me to realize, what do I know about miracles?
Of welcoming, fear, or "we"?
I live at the top of a hill.
Most days I do little real.

Instead, I watch trees move, cycles of seasons,
admire an appreciative horizon.
But I have learned from trees not to trust
what I see, like up into their canopy
a nest, fused limbs, gnarled evidence,
limped or clumped together. What falls.
Men act, live, die, get punished,

[. . .]

get away with it. I imagine this west wind
two thousand miles later,
descending into Minneapolis,
acting on faces at an intersection,
winding into ducts or sussing through windows,
brushing someone's face inside a courtroom
to at most blink at it.

Anything more concrete or more lasting,
that is up to all of us. That pulling of the world
toward us. All the four named winds,
with Boreas and Notus coming toward us,
together acting in swirling concert,
pushing tomorrow onto us.
What will we do?

What will I?
Air separates a gavel and its block,
prosecutor from defendant. Air
carries pronouncements of verdict,
carry voices for or against
through hallways and onto streets,
into the mind, the images, the readings, history.

There becomes here,
and from where we live, where I,
travel of significance has nothing to do
with the wind. The one air that mattered,
that of another breath in,
or of a gap between face and pavement,
a miracle of unweighting, of rising up again,

for the one man to whom it mattered,
that will never come.

Tantalus

> *Now he hangs, perennially consumed by thirst and hunger...*

The natural word is *almost*,
the cause indifferent as
early summer evenings,
the long light; some jay
with brake-shoe screech;
early fruit and single-minded
thoughts to find them
through thorns. Later they will
weigh to touch the ground
but you want them now,
greedy as the jay
shitting holly seeds down
to bounce on bricks of the yard
such they seem to come from the sun.
Always around you
consuming want and change.
It can take over
the senses, and sense. That you
won't get it exactly right,
or ever. The word threatens to *become*.
Or that you,
that no one, will. Only *almost*.

Medusa

> *...with what had been drawn from the veins of her left side, he could raise the dead; with what had been drawn from her right side, he could destroy instantly.*

I have never seen
coral of the Red Sea,
nor the Red Sea at night.

But I have seen coral
deadening indirect
from ways to transit of the sea

which constitutes the world
today. And I have seen
the sea at night,

its tenebrous quality
come up from depths
under the death of the sun—

there
is that beauty, unmasked,
revealing black.

Darkness quenches faith.
The Gorgon's blood said from one side
to raise the dead,

destroyer of all with the other,
discovery in the pursuit of glory—
no so-called hero

has yet stopped to ask
on the larger meaning of sacrifice:
that somewhere in the sand

might lay the simple question
waiting to be found:
do we need her?

the answer,
if allowed,
burrows deeper and deeper—

yes, we need her.

Acknowledgments

The poems in *Olympic* were the direct result of a series of generative writing workshops around the Greek myths led by Rebecca Smolen from spring through the fall of 2020. Within pandemic and election, fears of health and the republic, Rebecca's salons were a sanctuary and powerful means for expression. (https://rebeccawritespdx.squarespace.com)

Thank you to Bruce Parker and Diane Corson, co-founders and deep patrons of Portland Ars Poetica, for over six years of salons in their living room in North Portland. There, a dozen of us or more would hone a practice of companionship in close reading and revision that made for inevitably stronger work. Thank you as well to the friends—Noël Ponthieux, Saxar, the late Sam Seskin—who hosted salons and events that made for stronger community.

Thank you to the larger Portland literary community, without whom I would not be completely an author: to Dan Encarnacion, co-organizer with me on Free Range Poetry, a pre-pandemic monthly featured reading and open mic series in Portland, Oregon; to Willamette Writers (www.willamettewriters.org) where I was a board member for four years; and to Christopher Luna and Printed Matter Vancouver (https://printedmattervancouver.com) for the consistently good work I get out of The Work.

And thank you to the editors of the following publication, where a few of these poems originally appeared, sometimes under a different form or title:

Wax Poetry and Art: "Demeter"

West Trade Review: "Eris"

Notes about the Epigraphs

Richard Hugo excerpted from *The Triggering Town: Lectures and Essays on Poetry and Writing*, W.W. Norton & Company, Reissue edition 2010.

Torin Greathouse excerpted from "Medusa with the Head of Perseus," (https://www.poetryfoundation.org/poetrymagazine/poems/150926/medusa-with-the-head-of-perseus).

George Seferis excerpted from "King of Asine," as translated by Jennifer Kellogg, (https://chs.harvard.edu/jennifer-kellogg-george-seferis-and-homers-light).

All other epigraphs are quoted from Robert Graves, *The Greek Myths*, Penguin Classics Deluxe Edition. Penguin Publishing Group.

About the Author

John L. Miller's poetry was featured at the Elisabeth Jones Art Center's 2021 Festival of Feelings. His poetry has also appeared in *West Trade Review*, *Tiny Seed Literary Journal*, *Wingless Dreamer*, *Wax Poetry and Art*, *Third Wednesday: A Literary & Arts Journal*, Not a Pipe Publishing's anthology *Shout*, *River Heron Review*, *catheXis northwest press*, T*he Esthetic Apostle*, the 9Bridges anthology *Over Land and Rising*, and *Glass Facets of Poetry*. His short fiction has appeared in *Tethered by Letters*.

John is a founder of Portland Ars Poetica, a literary poetry collective serving the U.S. Pacific Northwest and when virtual, anywhere. Portland Ars Poetica's activities include generative workshops, a book club and performance events. More information on Portland Ars Poetica can be found at https://www.meetup.com/Portland-Ars-Poetica/

John has lived in Portland, Oregon since 2012, where he started to write poetry after writing almost nothing in verse for 20 years. A writer from as far back in childhood as he can remember and has files on, John was born and raised in Brooklyn, New York. He wrote his first poem at fifteen, on the New York City subway, on a bookmark that he placed in a copy of Paul Fussell's *The Great War and Modern Memory*, which remains on his shelves. He has a degree in English from Amherst College.

About The Poetry Box®

The Poetry Box, a boutique publishing company in Portland, Oregon, provides a platform for both established and emerging poets to share their words with the world through beautiful printed books and chapbooks.

Feel free to visit the online bookstore (thePoetryBox.com), where you'll find more titles including:

Exchanging Wisdom by Christopher & Angelo Luna

Sophia & Mister Walter Whitman by Penelope Scambly Schott

Dear John— by Laura LeHew

A Shape of Sky by Cathy Cain

Excoriation by Rebecca Smolen

Of the Forest by Linda Ferguson

What She Was Wearing by Shawn Aveningo Sanders

The Catalog of Small Contentments by Carolyn Martin

Tell Her Yes by Ann Farley

Sitting in Powell's Watching Burnside Dissolve in the Rain by Doug Stone

Beneath the Gravel Weight of Stars by Mimi German

A Nest in the Heart by Vivienne Popperl

and more . . .

www.ingramcontent.com/pod-product-compliance
Lightning Source LLC
LaVergne TN
LVHW020440080526
838202LV00055B/5280